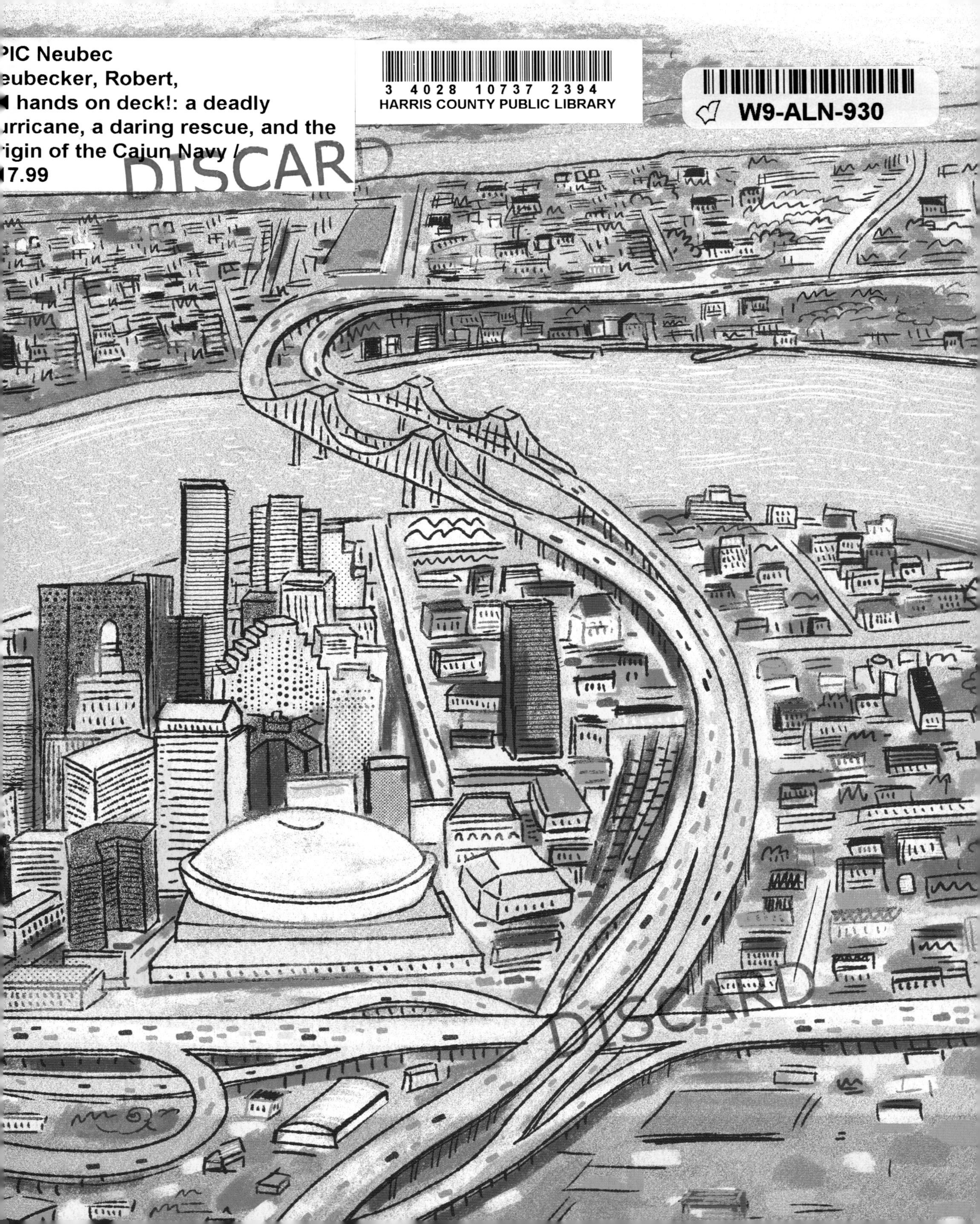

To the people of New Orleans

ALL HANDS ON DECK!

A DEADLY HURRICANE, A DARING RESCUE, AND THE ORIGIN OF THE CAJUN NAVY

ROBERT NEUBECKER

Alfred A. Knopf
New York

All kinds of boats cruise up and down the Gulf Coast, fishing and sailing and tugging.

Each little boat has its
own watery purpose.

Bubba is a bass boat.
He is small and quiet and loves to catch fish.
He fishes for bass in rivers and lakes.

BUBBA

BENNIE

Bennie is an airboat. He goes just about anywhere there's water. He lives in the shallows of the bayous and swamps.

Sal is a speedboat.
She is sleek and fast
and made for fun.

Water-skiers! Wakeboarders!
Zoom! Zoom!

Over the sea, a storm is brewing.
It gathers strength from the warm water
and grows bigger . . .

and bigger . . .

and bigger.

The ocean goes wild.
The wind screams and howls.

Hurricane!

It rains and rains. . . .

Some people leave the city.

But not everyone can get out.

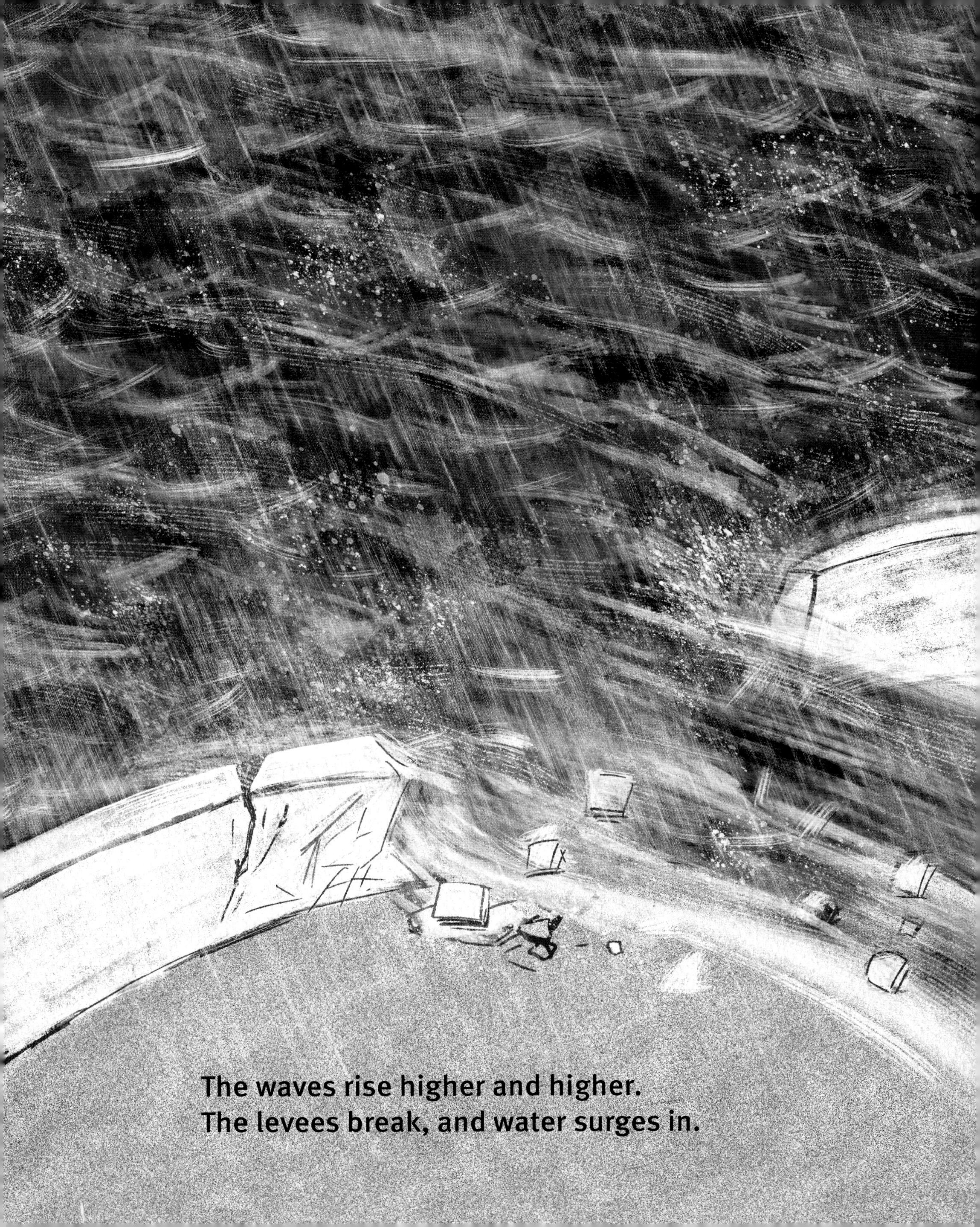

The waves rise higher and higher.
The levees break, and water surges in.

Firefighters, police, and the Coast Guard come to the rescue.

But there are too many people who must be saved.

Bubba worries.
“How can I help?
I’m just a little
fishing boat.”

Bennie is alarmed as
water floods the streets.
He wonders: “What can
one airboat do?”

Sal wishes
she could do
something.
“I’m not a hero.
I’m just a good-
time boat.”

Then the word goes out, over radio and TV.
“New Orleans is flooded.
Thousands of people are stranded!”

Bubba has an idea: “If all the little boats work together, we can do big things.”

Bennie thinks: “With my fan and shallow draft, I can go where no one else can.”

Sal says: “A fast boat could be the right boat. They may have a need for my speed.”

The little boats
come from all
over the coast,
one by one.

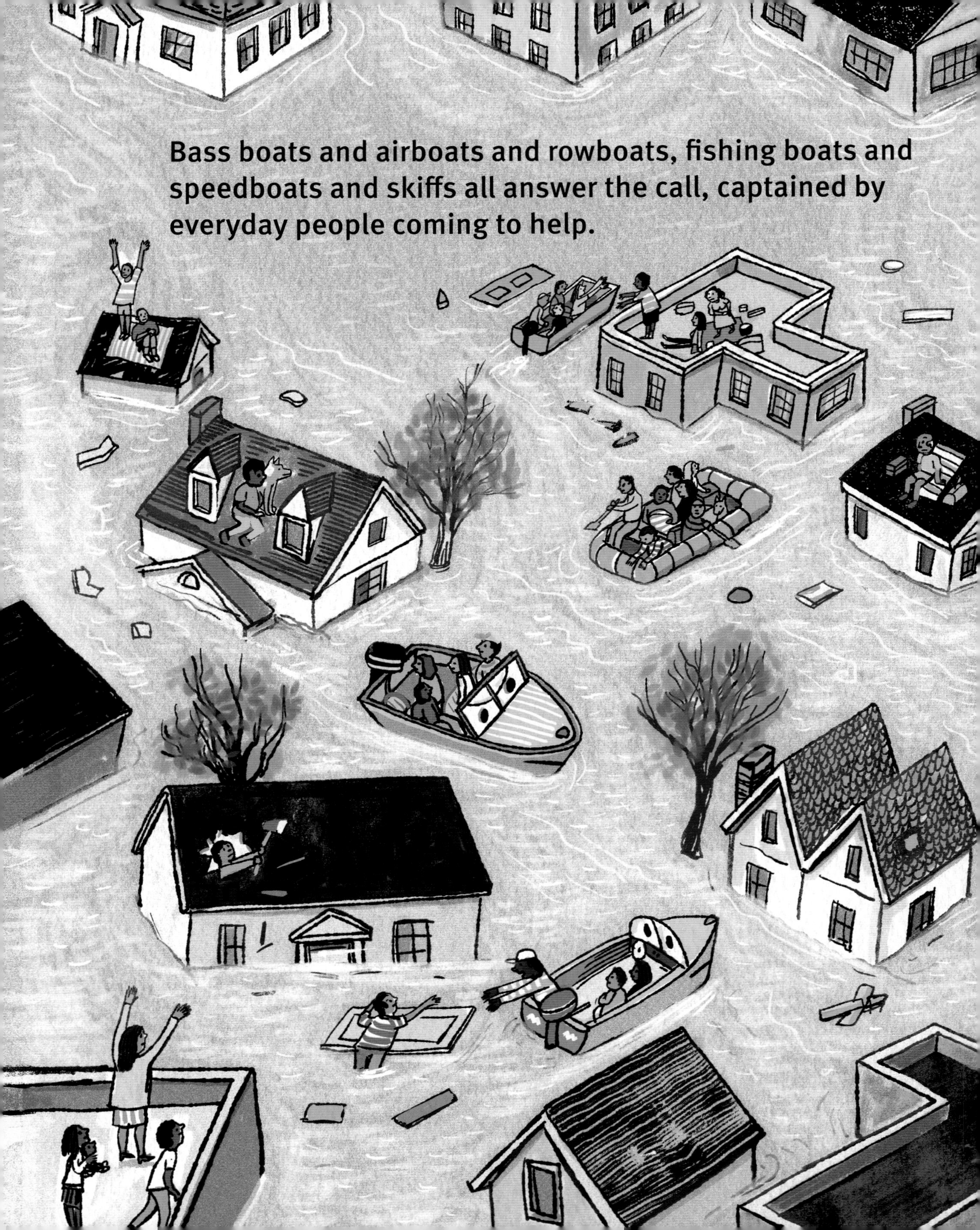

Bass boats and airboats and rowboats, fishing boats and speedboats and skiffs all answer the call, captained by everyday people coming to help.

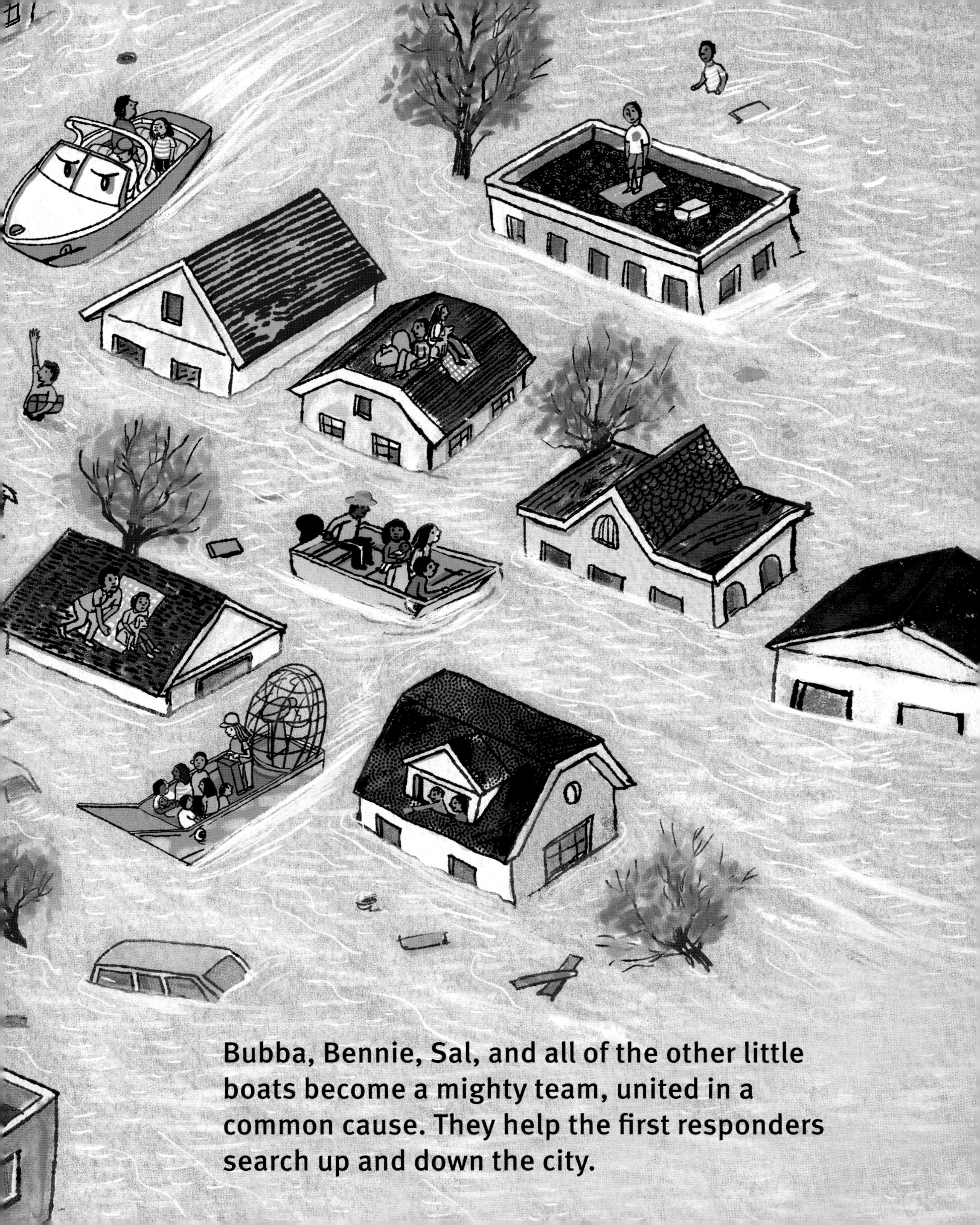

Bubba, Bennie, Sal, and all of the other little boats become a mighty team, united in a common cause. They help the first responders search up and down the city.

Bubba joins the other little boats to pluck people from rooftops.

Bennie goes in where no one else can.

Sal rushes from one emergency to the next.

They rescue little kids and grandparents, moms and dads, brothers and sisters, cats and dogs.

Together they save thousands of people.

The little boats and their owners come to be called "The Cajun Navy."

SAL
BUBBA

And the next time the sky grows dark and the sea goes wild, the Cajun Navy will be ready.

HURRICANES need warm water and wind to start. When ocean water warms to 80°F or more, wind blowing over the water causes it to evaporate and turn into vapor. The water vapor rises, forming thunderclouds. Wind blows these clouds in a circle, which grows and grows until it becomes a tropical disturbance.

More warm air rises, and the winds spin faster. When they reach 25–38 mph, the storm is called a tropical depression.

When the winds spin 39 mph or more, it's called a tropical storm.

When the winds blow at 74 mph and higher, you have a hurricane—the strongest storm on planet Earth.

HURRICANE CATEGORIES

Category	Wind Speed (mph)	Damage at Landfall
1	74–95	Minimal
2	96–110	Moderate
3	111–129	Extensive
4	130–156	Extreme
5	157 or higher	Catastrophic

HURRICANE KATRINA grew to a Category 5 hurricane over the Gulf of Mexico. When it made landfall along the Gulf Coast on August 29, 2005, it was still a strong Category 3, with winds reaching 120 mph. More than half of the levees protecting New Orleans broke, and 80% of the city was flooded.

The city was hit hard. Over a million people were displaced. Over 1,200 people died, and hundreds of thousands were left homeless. Thousands of refugees crowded into the Superdome, a giant covered stadium, where the heat and lack of food and water took more lives. At Hancock Medical Center, doctors worked tirelessly to save patients on the second floor while fish swam in the lobby and the roof was blown off of the third floor.

The government was caught unprepared, so all kinds of people turned out to help. The Coast Guard and first responders saved over 33,500 people. The National Guard and agencies like the Red Cross brought much-needed supplies. The Louisiana Society for the Prevention of Cruelty to Animals (LSPCA) saved more than 8,500 pets. And the Louisiana Department of Wildlife and Fisheries worked with the Cajun Navy and other volunteers to save thousands more lives.

THE CAJUN NAVY began when Sam Jones, from the Louisiana governor's office, called Sara Roberts, a member of the Superdome Commission, and asked her to gather volunteers with boats. They started out with just eighteen boats, but with former naval officer Ronnie Lovett leading the charge, soon there were hundreds. The Cajun Navy still exists today, and its members assist in search-and-rescue efforts all along the Gulf Coast. The next time a hurricane strikes, they'll be there to help!

HURRICANE SAFETY

If you live in a hurricane-prone area, it's important to have a disaster plan:

- Research local evacuation routes and decide on a meeting place if you become separated from your family.
- Prepare a disaster kit with enough canned food and bottled water to last three days, a first-aid kit, protective clothing, and a battery-operated flashlight and radio for weather updates. Don't forget to include a can opener and plenty of batteries!
- Remind your parents to keep some cash on hand, gas up the car, and unplug all appliances.
- Make a plan for your pets.
- Board up windows.
- Bring in all outdoor objects that could be blown away.

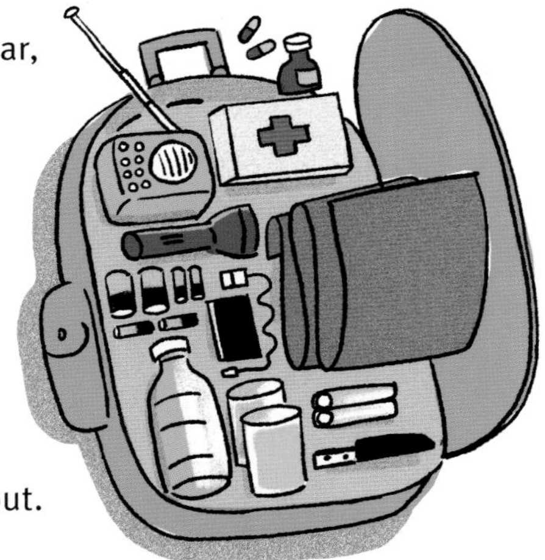

During a hurricane:

- Always stay indoors and away from windows.
- Go to a shelter if you live in a mobile home or flood zone.
- Evacuate immediately if directed by emergency managers.
- Stay inside until emergency managers say it's safe to come out. A period of calm may simply be the eye of the storm, with dangerous weather soon to return.
- Check for injured or trapped people while staying safe yourself.

THIS IS A BORZOI BOOK PUBLISHED BY ALFRED A. KNOPF

Library of Congress Cataloging-in-Publication Data
Names: Neubecker, Robert, author.
Title: All hands on deck! : a deadly hurricane, a daring rescue, and the origin of the Cajun Navy / Robert Neubecker.
Description: First edition. | New York : Alfred A. Knopf, 2021. | Audience: Ages 3–6. | Audience: Grades K–1. | Summary: When a terrible storm hits the Gulf Coast, Bubba the bass boat, Bennie the airboat, and Sal the speedboat are called upon to help rescue people and animals. Inspired by the true story of rescues during Hurricane Katrina and its aftermath. Includes facts about hurricanes and the Cajun Navy.
Identifiers: LCCN 2020025029 (print) | LCCN 2020025030 (ebook) | ISBN 978-0-593-17689-4 (hardcover) | ISBN 978-0-593-17690-0 (library binding) | ISBN 978-0-593-17691-7 (ebook)
Subjects: CYAC: Boats and boating—Fiction. | Rescues—Fiction. | Hurricane Katrina, 2005—Fiction.
Classification: LCC PZ7.N4394 All 2021 (print) | LCC PZ7.N4394 (ebook) | DDC [E]—dc23
The illustrations in this book were created using watercolors, pencils, and a Mac.
MANUFACTURED IN CHINA May 2021 10 9 8 7 6 5 4 3 2 1 First Edition

NEWS